FAMILIES
BELONG

Families belong
Together like a puzzle
Different-sized people
One big snuggle

Fitting just so
Together.

Families sing
With voices bellowing
Songs that make us giggle
On the back of Dad's bicycle

Making melodies
Together.

Families gather
Around a heaping platter
Of favorite foods to
share . . .

. . . but some fell on the chair!

Cleaning up the crumbs
Together.

Families relax
On blankets in the grass
Listening to the wind
Not saying anything

Just being nice and still
Together.

Families spin
When thunderclouds roll in

The rumbling sounds like drums
Our party has begun

Dancing hand in hand
Together.

For Joni and Shiloh
—DS

For Eliza, Finn and Remy
—BS

The publisher does not have any control over and does not assume any responsibility for author or third-party websites or their content.

Text copyright © 2020 by Dan Saks. Illustrations copyright © 2020 by Brooke Smart. All rights reserved. Published by by Rise x Penguin Workshop, an imprint of Penguin Random House LLC, New York. PENGUIN and PENGUIN WORKSHOP are trademarks of Penguin Books Ltd. The W colophon is a registered trademark and the RISE colophon is a trademark of Penguin Random House LLC. Manufactured in China.

The text is set in Futura Std.
The art was created with watercolor and gouache and edited in Photoshop.

Edited by Cecily Kaiser
Designed by Maria Elias

LCCN: 2019056139
ISBN 9780593222768
Special Markets ISBN 9780593384145 Not for Resale
10 9 8 7 6 5 4 3 2 1

This Imagination Library edition is published by Penguin Young Readers, a division of Penguin Random House, exclusively for Dolly Parton's Imagination Library, a not-for-profit program designed to inspire a love of reading and learning, sponsored in part by The Dollywood Foundation. Penguin's trade editions of this work are available wherever books are sold.

Together.

Families belong

Love together

In any weather

We laugh together
Cry together

Play together
Try together

Together.

Families care
When no one else is there
In unfamiliar places
We're making funny faces